Frederick Lowey, William Lowey

The Art of Gold, Silver, Nickel and Copper Plating Made Easy

Frederick Lowey, William Lowey

The Art of Gold, Silver, Nickel and Copper Plating Made Easy

ISBN/EAN: 9783337392932

Printed in Europe, USA, Canada, Australia, Japan

Cover: Foto ©Andreas Hilbeck / pixelio.de

More available books at **www.hansebooks.com**

Price Twenty-Five Cents.

THE ART OF
GOLD, SILVER, NICKEL
—AND—
COPPER PLATING
MADE EASY.

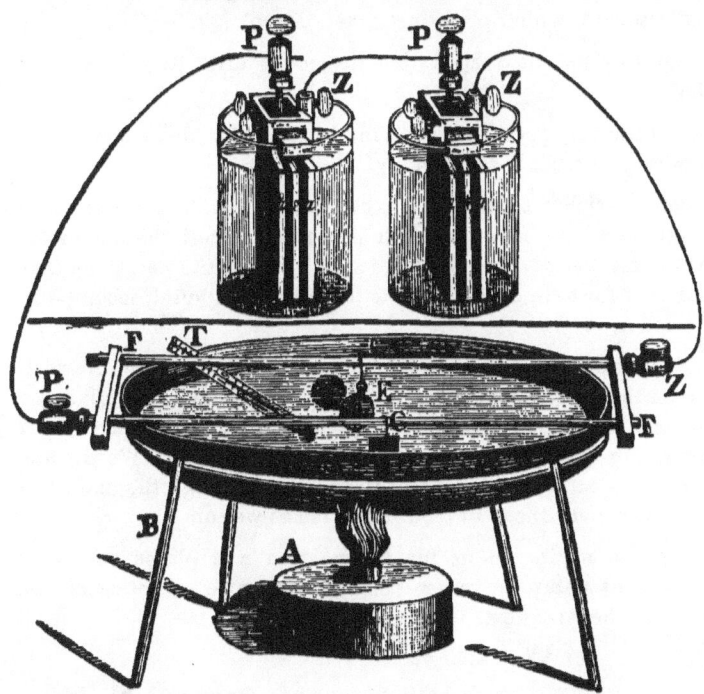

**Two of Wm. Lowey's Improved SMEE'S Batteries, connected.
with Gilding Pan in the act of Gilding a Watch-Case.**

NEW YORK:
PUBLISHED BY
WILLIAM LOWEY,
MANUFACTURER OF
Electro-Platers' Batteries & Supplies, of all kinds,
85 NASSAU STREET.

NOTICE.

Parties ordering goods should send money by post office order or registered letter, or by draft on New York, made payable to William Lowey, as it is not safe to trust money in ordinary letters.

All monies sent otherwise will be at sender's risk.

Cash *must* accompany *all* orders. Goods will be sent C. O. D. only when one-half the amount is sent with the order, to insure good faith.

All goods will be packed with the greatest care, and the price of the box added to the bill in all cases except in the small plating batteries, which prices are given boxed.

We will not be responsible for goods after they leave our office.

In ordering goods to be sent by express, please state what express you wish them sent by.

Small articles, such as wire, connections, salts, powders and small zincs can be sent much cheaper by mail than express. Where articles of this class are sent by mail it is necessary that one cent for each ounce, or fraction thereof, should accompany the order.

N. B. Parties buying goods from us, and having trouble with the batteries, or in their work, if they will write to us, giving a description of their trouble, we will look into the matter for them, and let them know the cause of the trouble. We do not purpose to carry on a course of instruction through the mail, but simply to help those in trouble, as far as we can.

Parties writing to us for information will please enclose a three cent stamp for return postage, otherwise no notice will be taken of their request.

W. LOWEY,
85 Nassau Street, N. Y.

TH... T

Gold, Sil... Nickel

COPPE... ING

M A D ... S Y .

A C... ...ESS

Out of Darkness Into Light.

THINK IT OVER.

READ THIS INTRODUCTION CAREFULLY.

The art of Electroplating is an invention of modern date, and has hitherto been kept in the hands of a few, who have monopolized the whole business. But now an opportunity is offered for all to acquire this very simple and lucrative business. There is scarcely a town or village in the United States but would give sufficient employment for at least one operator. The uses of electroplating are constantly extending.

To meet a want, long felt, is the design of the publisher of this little manual, who can well remember the trouble he had when a boy to get the apparatus required to perform simple experiments in chemistry. No small or cheap sets of apparatus were then known, and not having a pocketful of money he had to construct his own. Having to make oxygen gas at one time, and having no apparatus at hand, he took the chimney from a lamp, put a cork in the upper end of it, then taking a basin of water he filled the chimney with water and inverted it in the basin; to generate the gas, he took a three-drachm vial and half-filled it with chlorate of potash and peroxide of manganese in about equal proportions; having placed a small glass tube in a cork he placed the cork in the bottle, and taking a small rubber tube he connected the bottle with the mouth of the chimney.

Everything was now ready; taking the small bottle up in his hand he held it over a kerosene lamp, and in a few moments the gas came bubbling over into the chimney, displacing the water in it, and in a few minutes it was full of gas. Now taking a small piece of cork, he placed upon it a little piece of phosphorus, and touched it with a hot wire, which ignited it; then he lifted up the chimney and placed it over the cork, and the result was a light of dazzling brilliancy. This is one of the most brilliant experiments that is performed upon the lecture table. In this way he had to proceed in all his studies. So that he is able to fully appreciate the difficulties which young students have to encounter in their studies, and will ever hold himself ready to help them, not only in selecting apparatus but also in showing them how they can construct their own, and thus save their money. It is his cherished desire to foster in the youth of this country a stronger desire for scientific studies, to take the place of the light and vile matter which publishers are spreading broadcast over the land, and which is killing both morals and mind of the rising generation.

For this purpose the publisher is getting up sets of cheap apparatus, with which any one can perform some of the most brilliant and beautiful experiments known in natural and chemical philosophy, that they may become so interested in the study that one experiment will drag them into another, until finally they will have brought themselves through a thorough course of study in the natural sciences.

It was this that prompted him to make these small batteries, so that boys and even men might take hold of them and learn the whole ins and outs of one of the most interesting as well as profitable trades. With one of these batteries any one with ordinary brains can set to work and plate knives, forks, spoons, rings, and various other small articles, to the intense interest of the whole family, who are gathered around to see the article gradually assume a silvery white appearance, and who wonder why it is they cannot see the little grains of silver flying through the solution to fasten itself on the article. With these batteries can be made all kinds of cheap jewelry the same as that now sold in such quantities over the whole country.

Now where money is an object this is just the thing. Where is there a place that will not support at least one silverplater, to say nothing of the large cities, which can support hundreds. Then there is electrotyping, a trade that pays in this city to a good electrotyper $40 and even $50 a week, and they are hard to get even at that money. Now what is there to prevent you from studying up this subject with one of these small batteries? You will have everything that is necessary to go through the whole operation of an electrotype foundry, or gold silver, and nickel plating, or the manufacture of jewelry, only on a small scale. You can get as good an impression as they can, only not so large. Thus, with a little practice you will be able to fill a lucrative position in some silverplating establishment or electrotyping foundry. This is a business very easily learned, is light, easily started in, and pays largely. Such offers as this have never been made before.

THINK OVER IT, and see if it will not pay you to send for one of these batteries. Do not be afraid to write to us, for nothing will please us half so well as to know that we have been the means of helping some person along.

To the Older People.

We are constantly receiving letters from our correspondents, inquiring whether we think it would pay for them to go into the electroplating business, or the manufacture of cheap jewelry, stating the towns or cities they reside in, and the number of inhabitants, and whether we think they could learn the art. To all these inquiries we would say that electroplating is very profitable, and can be learned by any person of ordinary intelligence,- especially by parties who have a knowledge of working in metals to perfection, as locksmiths, jewellers, silversmiths, gunsmiths, sewing-machine makers, and plumbers, and in fact any business where work is required to look well.

We would recommend our plating sets, as the business is very profitable and can be done in a very small room, and will not interfere with other work. There are hundreds that send their work by express to distant cities to be plated. The expense and delay can all be avoided by doing your own plating, and you can do it better and cheaper yourself, because you know just how much metal you have on the work.

We have sent our plating sets to parties who knew nothing about plating, and with the assistance of our book they were successful beyond their expectations, and from a small beginning they have built up a large business. There is not a city or town in the United States and Canadas in which there cannot be a good business done in jobbing, such as plating watches, tea sets. tea pitchers, knives and forks, etc.

We should advise parties who intend to start a jobbing shop or manufactory, to get the silver plating set described elsewhere, as that includes everything that is necessary to commence with; then as work increases and they become experts in the art, they can enlarge this apparatus so as to meet the requirements of their work. The $40.00 set will silver plate a tea set, castors, spoons, knives, forks, etc. For jewellers and watchmakers we would recommend the $32.00 set, as jewellers' work is not so large, and they would not require so much battery power.

W. LOWEY,

MANUFACTURER AND DEALER IN

GOLD, SILVER, AND NICKEL PLATERS' BATTERIES,

AND PLATING MATERIALS OF ALL KINDS,

85 Nassau Street, New York.

THE ART OF GOLD, SILVER, AND NICKEL PLATING.

THE THEORY OF THE ELECTROTYPE PROCESS.

The electrotype process may be defined generally as the art of depositing metals upon suitable surfaces by means of a current of voltaic electricity. What voltaic electricity is, and how it acts in producing metallic deposits, may be easily shown by a few simple experiments.

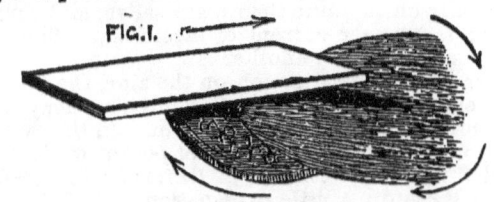

FIG. I.

Place a clean slip of zinc—say a couple of inches long and an inch wide—upon your tongue, and a silver coin—a dime for instance—under it, taking care not to let the metals touch each other. As long as the coin and the zinc are separated, no perceptible effect is produced ; but allow them to touch each other, as shown in Fig. 1, and you will experience a peculiar tingling sensation in the tongue, accompanied by a metallic or saline taste. These sensations are repeated as often as the two metals are joined or separated.

In this simple experiment lies the whole principle of the production of voltaic electricity, and the effects experienced depends on the following laws:

I. Whenever two different metals are placed in a liquid and joined, electricity is generated on the surface of that metal which is most easily acted upon by the liquid, and flows toward the other. For example, in the present case the zinc is more easily acted upon by the saliva then the silver, the consequence being that a current of electricity starts from the surface of the zinc, travels through the saliva and the tongue to the silver, and so round to the zinc again, in the direction of the arrows in Fig. 1. In passing through the tongue, the current stimulates the nerves of that organ, and slightly decomposes the saliva, giving rise to the sensations already described.

It will be as well to impress firmly on your mind the course taken by the current, as you will find this knowledge exceedingly useful in future experiments. The positions of the metals may of course be reversed without in any way altering the effects of the experiment.

By varying this simple experiment in one or two ways, we may gain a little more information on the subject.

Wash the mouth out with salt and water, and repeat the experiment. You will now find that the sensations you formerly felt are increased, owing to the fact of the salt and water acting more energetically on the zinc than plain saliva, and consequently producing a stronger current of electricity. This experiment enables us to lay down another law:

II. The stronger the chemical action on the zinc, the greater is the amount of electricity produced. Secondly, we may substitute a piece of gold or lead for the silver coin. In the case of the gold, we shall find an *increase* of electrical power, while with the lead we shall find, on the contrary, a *decrease*. The reason of these changes will require a little explanation.

I have before said, and we have found it to be true by the first experiment, that when zinc is acted upon by a liquid it throws off a current of electricity. Now, this is not only true of zinc, but also of iron, lead, silver, gold, and all other metals, but to a much less extent. When, therefore, a plate of lead is used with the zinc, the saliva acts on both, a *strong* current of electricity being set up by the zinc, and an opposition *weak* one by the lead; the real value of the zinc current is consequently reduced by that flowing from the lead. With silver, the opposition current is still less, silver being only very slightly influenced by the saliva; while with gold, which is practically unaffected, we obtain the zinc current in its fullest intensity, with scarcely any diminution or drawback.

We can now lay down a third law:

III. That the most energetic effect is produced when the two metals used differ as widely as possible in their capacity for being acted upon by the liquid in which they are immersed.

The following list of common metals, arranged in the order in which they are acted upon by dilute sulphuric acid, will enable us to see this a little more clearly:

GOLD......................................Imperceptibly.
PLATINUM.................................Hardly at all.
SILVER.............................Very slightly indeed.
COPPER...... ....Very slightly.
TIN...Slightly.
LEAD...........................Somewhat strongly.
IRON...Strongly.
ZINC..................................Very strongly.
POTASSIUM....................Very strongly indeed.

If, therefore, we wish to make the strongest possible voltaic pair that the above metals will afford, we should use gold and potassium ; but as these metals are exceedingly dear, we use zinc in combination with platinum, silver, or copper, according to circumstances.

There is one substance, however, which beats even gold when used with zinc, and that is carbon or charcoal, which, although not a metal, acts as one in a voltaic combination. This may be tried by using a piece of well-burned charcoal instead of a silver coin, as in our first experiment.

Here, then, we have all the conditions heretofore laid down for forming a voltaic pair :

First, a plate of metal, such as zinc, which is easily acted on chemically ; secondly, another plate of metal, such as platinum, silver, or copper, which is attacked with great difficulty ; thirdly, a liquid such as saliva, water, solution of salt, or of some acid, to act upon the zinc ; and lastly, a vessel of some kind—preferably *not* the mouth—to contain the whole.

These conditions are admirably fulfilled in the zinc and platinized silver battery which is known by the name of its inventor, Mr. Alfred Smee, of which the following is a description :

SMEE BATTERY.

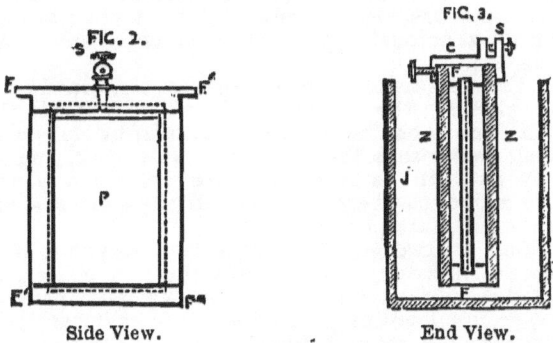

Side View.　　　　　　　　End View.

Fig. 2 is a frame, F F' F" F"', containing a sheet of platinized silver, P, to which is attached a binding screw, S (not shown in Fig. 3), into which may be fastened a wire. Fig. 3 shows the frame in section, with the zinc plates attached. Z Z are the zinc plates, (not shown in Fig. 2,) which are kept in their places by the clamp, C (not shown in Fig. 2). On the top of the clamp is another binding screw, S', which serves to hold another wire. The whole is immersed in the jar, J (not shown in Fig. 2), which contains sulphuric acid and water.

Here we have the perfect representation of the voltaic pair we formed in the first experiment, only we have a convenient vessel instead of our mouth, and solution of sulphuric acid instead of saliva. We also have the power of prolonging our plates by means of binding screws and wires, so that we may lead the force generated by the zinc in any direction we please. For instance, if you place the two wires in your mouth, you will notice the same sensations as in our first experiment, but in an increased degree.

It may possibly puzzle you to understand why two plates of zinc are used instead of only one, and also how it is that the current only passes when the zinc and silver plates are connected. The following explanation will make this clear to you.

When a plate of zinc is immersed—say, in dilute acid—electricity is immediately generated on both of its surfaces; but if there be nothing to collect and convey this electricity away, it remains where it is. If, however, a plate of some other metal is placed in the liquid, it collects the electricity generated by the zinc; but even now the current will not flow except communication through a conductor be made between the plate and the zinc.

Going back to our first experiment, let us see what happened. You first laid the zinc on your tongue; but although chemical action took place, you felt no electrical current, neither did you when the dime was placed under it; and it was not until the dime and the zinc touched that you experienced any manifestation of electricity.

As it is the surfaces of the plates that are concerned in generating or collecting the current produced, we prefer in the battery I am describing to make the platinized silver—which is very much dearer than the zinc—do double work, and collect electricity on both its surfaces. We consequently use two plates of zinc, so that there may be electricity generated on both sides of the platinum plate.

Here, then, are two more important facts for you to recollect: first, that no electricity passes until the two plates are connected, either by their free ends, as in our first experiment, or by wires, as in all ordinary batteries, when it instantly begins circling round and round until all the zinc is dissolved, or the acid becomes so weak as to act on it no longer; secondly, that it is on the *surface* of the zinc next the inactive collecting plate that the current of electricity is produced. In the present instance we might make one zinc plate give out electricity from both of its surfaces by using two plates of platinized silver; but as that material is worth some hundred times as much as the zinc, it is better, as I have before said, to make the dear material do the double work.

It is hardly necessary for me to say that the amount of electrical effect that may be produced by a zinc plate is entirely in proportion to its surface, and has nothing to do with its thickness. Thus the thin platinized silver plate is just as effective as if it were half an inch thick. In the case of the zinc, we use pretty thick plates, simply because they take longer to dissolve away than thin ones.

The ordinary commercial zinc used for batteries is very impure. It contains numerous particles of lead, iron, and carbon, which set up little opposition voltaic currents on their own account as soon as the plate is immersed in the acid. To obviate this, the zinc has to undergo the process of amalgamation by being rubbed over with mercury before it is fit for use. The mercury forms with the zinc a semi-fluid compound, which spreads over the surface, and covers up the little particles of other metals, and prevents them from being acted on by the acid. The process of amalgamating the zinc is very simple, and will be described further on.

Having now made ourselves pretty well acquainted with the construction and action of the voltaic battery, we will make a few experiments on its effects. In our first experiment we found that the saliva on our tongue was slightly decomposed. The decomposition of substances through which the current passes is one of the most characteristic effects of the voltaic battery. The Smee's pair, already described, has hardly power enough to effect the decomposition of water—that is to say, to separate it into its component gases, oxygen and hydrogen; but there are other substances so easy of decomposition that we may decompose them with our slip of zinc and dime.

Dissolve a few crystals of sulphate of copper, which is composed of copper, oxygen, and sulphuric acid, in a cup of water; throw into it a silver coin, and leave it there for a few moments. On lifting it out, the coin is as bright as it was before. But create an electric current through the sulphate of copper solution by touching the coin with a slip of zinc as it lies at the bottom of the cup, and you will shortly find a deposit of metallic copper covering the silver. By immersing the zinc in the sulphate of copper solution we have created a current of electricity, which passes through the liquid, decomposing it, the copper going to the silver, and the other components of the sulphate of copper —sulphuric acid and oxygen—going to the zinc, which is gradually dissolved.

Now we may do precisely the same thing with our Smee's pair. We may conduct the electricity generated by means of wires into a solution of sulphate of copper, and decompose it, one wire becoming coated with copper like the dime, and the other becoming oxidized, and dissolving in the liberated sulphuric acid.

Next we may attach to one wire a coin, to the other a piece of copper, to supply the place of that deposited on the coin, and we may allow the current to pass until the deposit on the coin is thick enough to remove; or, lastly. we may substitute for the coin a wax mould, made conductible by black lead, and so obtain an electrotype copy of it in copper.

Here, then, we have the whole theory of electrotyping, and we have arrived at it in a truly philosophical manner, beginning with one simple experiment with the zinc and dime, and working gradually onwards step by step.

I will now describe to you what is known as the single-cell Daniell's battery—a form of voltaic combination much used by beginners.

It may have occurred to you while endeavoring to coat your dime with copper that a piece of zinc, with a wire attached to it carrying a black-leaded mould, might be immersed in a jar of sulphate of copper solution, and constitute a rude electrotype apparatus. Such an idea would be perfectly correct in theory, but in practice you would find that the zinc itself would in turn become coated with copper, and that very soon all action would cease. Provide some means, however, by which the zinc would be protected from the action of the sulphate of copper, and we get a very efficient apparatus for ordinary purposes. The following is a description of the ordinary single-cell Daniell, which is so much used for electrotyping small objects. But I would advise you most strongly to put your trust entirely in Smee. The Daniell is certainly cheaper at first, but the continual break age of porous pots, and the uncertainty with which it works, render it dearer in the end.

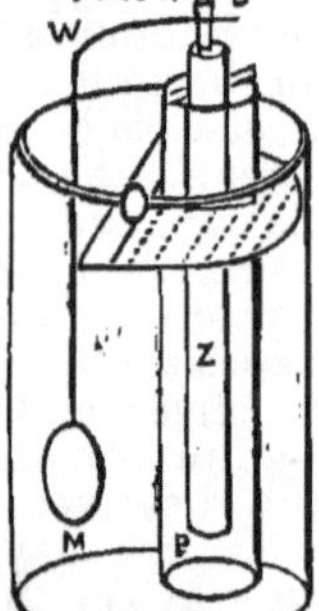

It consists (Fig. 4) of a jar, J, containing a porous pot, P, within which is placed a cylinder of zinc. Z, To this is attached by means of a binding screw, B, a wire, W, carrying the black-leaded mould, M. The outer jar is filled with a solution of sulphate of copper, and porous pot with dilute sulphuric acid. You will, no doubt, at once think that this cannot be a voltaic pair generating a current of electricity, there being no inactive plate to collect the electricity developed by the zinc; but a little reflection will show you that the black-leaded mould is the collecting plate in this instance, becoming covered with copper as long as the current flows. A little more reflection is liable to raise a new difficulty as to the possibility of the electricity generated by the zinc passing through the porous pot, which is a non-conducting material; but if we only consider that the two liquids pass through the pores of the clay, and mix together very slowly, the difficulty vanishes. .

FIG. 4.

One more explanation, and I am done with theory. In using the Smee with a separate cell, it often puzzles one to know upon which wire to hang the mold ; but if we only take the trouble to trace the course of the current, and to recollect that it is at that particular spot where the current *leaves* the liquid that the metal is deposited, you will have no difficulty in remembering to which wire to attach your mould.

The following diagrams show the course taken by the current in the electrotyping arrangements that we have been considering, beginning with the zinc and dime.

In Figure 5 it begins at the zinc, passes through the sulphate of copper solution into the coin, leaving a deposit of copper behind it, and so upwards into the zinc again.

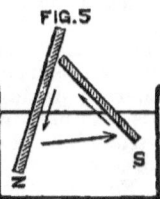

FIG.5

In Fig. 6 it begins with the zinc, and travels through the sulphuric acid solution, sulphate of copper, black-leaded mould, copper wire, and binding screw, to the zinc once more.

FIG. 6

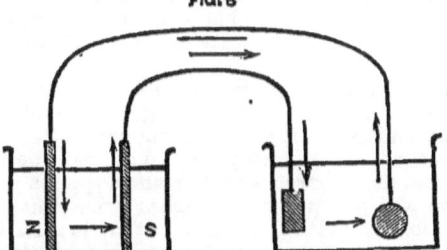

Let us now sum up the theory of the electrotype process.

I.—When a plate of zinc is immersed in a liquid which acts upon it chemically, electricity is developed on the surface of the metal.

II.—If you place opposite to the zinc another metal only slightly acted on by the liquid, and connect it with the zinc by means of a wire, the electricity developed by the zinc is set in motion, and a current is generated which lasts until chemical action ceases,

III.—When a current of electricity is passed through a liquid, the liquid is decomposed, provided the current is sufficiently strong.

IV.—If the solution through which the current passes contains a metal, it will be deposited at the point where the current passes out of the solution.

V.—the electric current will pass with more or less facility through all metals, charcoal, black lead, and most liquids, but nearly all other substances interrupt its passage. Bodies of the first kind are called conductors, the rest non-conductors. So much for the theory of the electrotype process, without some knowledge of which no one can hope to succeed in obtaining good results.

THE PRACTICE.

One of the first things the electrotyper will have to practise is the art of making moulds of the objects he wishes to reproduce. When first the electrotype process was discovered, the electrotyper was obliged to confine himself to the use of moulds in metal, it being erroneously supposed that deposition would only take place on metallic surfaces; the discovery, however, that any surface well rubbed with plumbago or black lead was thereby made conducting, freed the art at once from many of its trammels and enabled the operator to use almost any material that would take a sharp impression of the object he desired to copy.

For seals, coins, and medals, nothing is better than ordinary white wax of good quality mixed with a little flake white. We will suppose, if you please, that you are desirous of making a copy of the Goddess of Liberty on the back of the fifty cent piece.

The first thing to do is to procure *good wax*. The common white wax sold at the oil-stores is generally adulterated with tallow or fat, and is a soft yielding material, utterly unfitted for the purposes of the electrotyper. You had better purchase your wax from the apparatus maker who supplies you with your battery; you will pay perhaps a higher price, but you will have the satisfaction of getting an article that is reliable. This remark will apply to nearly all the materials that you are likely to use.

As a rule, wax works much better when mixed with about one-twentieth of its weight of flake white, which may be purchased at an oil-store very cheaply. Put the wax into an ordinary earthen pipkin, and place it near a rather low, clear fire, free from smoke, taking care that the heat is only just sufficient to allow the wax to melt. When quite liquid throw in one-twentieth of its weight of flake white, and stir the whole with a glass rod or clean tobacco-pipe stem. When fully mixed pour the wax out on a clean plate, and, when cool, chop it up into little pieces and re-melt it. Repeat the cooling and melting once more, and the mixture is ready for use. You need not be particular about adhering to the exact proportions of wax and flake white given above; for instance, a quarter of a pound of the former and a quarter of an ounce of the latter form an excellent compound, are easy quantities to purchase, and consequently save the trouble of weighing. Of course it is better to make a large quantity of the mixture at once and keep it in cakes ready for use.

The coin from which you are about to take a cast should be rubbed over with a small quantity of sweet oil, taking care that it penetrates into all the finer parts of the work. As much as possible of the superfluous oil is then removed with a pledget of cotton wool the fine details being cleared with an ordinary sable or camel's hair pencil. The object of oiling the medal is to prevent the wax from sticking to it by the interposition of a very thin film of greasy matter.

You next surround the coin with a slip of thin card, about an inch or an inch and a half in width, and of sufficient length to overlap about an inch. Wrapping the card round the coin, mark with a pencil the line where the edge overlaps. You now tack together the top and bottom of the cardboard hoop with a needle and thread, so as to form a little cell for the reception of the coin, which will be retained in its place by the natural spring of the card. If the coin is heavy it will be better to wind some thread round the whole, so as to make assurance doubly sure. It is almost unnecessary to warn you against touching the face of the coin with the finger, as you will no doubt have guessed that the slightest mark will appear in the electrotype copy.

Having melted sufficient wax for the purpose you require, heat the coin by placing it on the stove, or holding it over a gas or candle flame, until it is just warm enough to prevent the hot wax from being suddenly chilled when poured upon it, and yet it must not be so hot as to dissipate the film of oil with which it is covered. The coin is now held steadily in the left hand and slightly sloping in that direction, in order that the melted wax may flow over the surface evenly and gradually. Pour in the wax gently and continuously until it rises nearly to the top of the cardboard. The whole is now put aside to cool, an operation that will take at least two hours; in fact, it is almost better to make the moulds over night and allow them to cool until the next morning. When the wax has become solid the threads fastening the card may be snipped and the cardboard peeled off —the mould, with the coin adhering to it, being placed aside in a cold place.

At first you will find some difficulty in getting perfect impressions, but the failure can only result from three causes. First, air bubbles may be formed through the coin being too cold, pouring the wax with an unsteady hand, or from too great a height; secondly, the wax may adhere to the mold so firmly as to resist all endeavors to separate them without destroying the impression, a misfortune that can only arise from not having left sufficient oil upon the coin; thirdly, the impression may be blurred and indistinct through the use of too much oil.

An excellent way to obtain a good impression of a coin, medal or like object, which will be found less tedious, is to melt your wax in a shallow vessel; set it aside to cool; meanwhile oil your object. When the wax has become pretty hard lay the object on the wax and squeeze it down with a carpenter's clamp. In this way we have obtained good sharp impressions.

Having perfected yourself in the art of casting from metal you should next try to cast from plaster. This is a somewhat difficult operation, but it is one to be learned—plaster copies of some of the finest works in the way of coins and medals being procurable at the Italian image-shops for a few cents. Having everything ready for casting, place the plaster impression, face upwards, in a saucer containing sufficient hot water to rise to half the height of the cast. Watch the surface of the plaster until it just begins to look wet. It is then taken out of the water, surrounded with cardboard, as in the case of the coin, and cast from in precisely the same way. Here, again, judgment is required; for if the plaster is made too wet the impression will be blurred, if it has sucked up too little water it will absorb the wax when poured upon it. Some electrotypers saturate the plaster with oil, but this method, although good for casting, spoils the appearance of the original cast. However, the best thing to do is to experiment upon both processes and choose the one that gives the best result.

If you cannot get the cake wax a good substitute will be found in wax candles; this will be found easy to work in as the mold does not stick so much.

Before commencing electrotyping it will be as well for you to practise casting until you have acquired the method of producing good impressions of all sizes, and from both plaster and metal. In fact you may accumulate casts during the time that you are saving up your dimes to buy your apparatus. Too many beginners electrotype from bad casts, the results being of course bad copies, to say nothing of the waste of time and material.

Your next step will be to set your battery at work. In all probability the zinc plates will have been amalgamated by the maker; but whether they have or not, it will be as well for you to perform the process upon them.

Make a mixture of one part by measure of sulphuric acid and four of water, taking care to pour in the acid last. The acid must be poured into the water very gently, otherwise so much heat is produced that the mixture spirts over the hands and clothes. Sulphuric acid, or oil of vitriol, as it is generally called, is exceedingly poisonous and corrosive. Whatever it falls upon it destroys; and although there is but little fear of any person drinking it, it should always be kept strictly under lock and key,

The mixture of sulphuric acid and water having become cold —for no matter how cautiously you pour the acid in, a certain amount of heat will always be generated—pour it into a plate or saucer, and place the zinc plates in it for half a minute or so if the plate has been amalgamated, or for a longer time if it has not. In the latter case, it should remain in the acid until it looks pretty clear. You will do well to notice the little bubbles that form upon the zinc, and rise to the surface in thousands. These are caused by numberless little voltaic pairs that are formed between the zinc and the particles of foreign metals with which it it is contaminated. Every one of these decomposes the water into oxygen and hydrogen, the former gas uniting with the zinc and becoming dissolved in the acid liquid, and the latter effervescing off in little bubbles like champagne. This does not occur with zinc which has been amalgamated. The zinc is lifted out of the acid, and a small quantity of mercury is poured upon it and gently rubbed over the surface with a piece of rag, taking care not to let the acid touch the fingers, for although it will not do them any harm, it is apt to produce dirty stains that take a long time wearing out. You may, if you like, make a little rubber by stuffing a piece of rag into a clean to-bacco pipe bowl, reserving the stem for stirring your solution. As soon as the zinc is perfectly bright in every part the super-fluous mercury should be removed with the rubber, and the plate washed in clean water and wiped. It generally happens that with new plates there are certain spots that will not amal-gamate, in which case the plate should be returned to the acid solution until they take the mercury as readily as any other part. It often puzzles young beginners to know when these plates wants re-amalgamating : to this query one might really reply by saying—always; in fact, the zinc plates used by some of the electric telegraph companies always stand in a little gutta-percha trough of mercury, so that the metal very gradually creeps up their surfaces; You may easily tell if a plate requires re-amalgamation or not by lifting it out of the cell, washing it in plenty of cold water, and pouring on it, when dry, a few drops of mercury. If the mercury flows readily over the surface the plate is still in working order; if, on the contrary, the mer-cury refuses to unite with the zinc, you may know that re-amal-gamation is necessary.

For using the battery, two solutions are required—one solution of sulphuric acid, for creating chemical action, and, consequent-ly, electricity on the surface of the zinc; the other a so-lution of sulphate of copper, from which we are to draw our supply of metal for covering our mould.

The acid solution for exciting the zinc is made by mixing one measure of sulphuric acid with twelve of water, care being taken to add the acid last, as when you were amalgamating. An egg cup forms an excellent measure for this purpose, and any quan-tity may be made at a time by adhering to the proportions given above. It is a good thing to keep a stock in hand, in a large bottle, so that the acid solution in the battery may be changed at a moment's notice. Some operators have a slovenly habit of pouring strong acid into the spent solution, the result being that they get themselves into most unexpected difficulties. When the exciting solution is exhausted, it should be thrown away and replaced· from your stock. Sulphuric acid is very cheap, a pound weight of it being sufficient to make five pints of solution.

The sulphate of copper solution is made by pouriug boiling water on a quantity of the salt—say a pint of the former upon a pound of the latter. The solution should be well stirred with a glass rod or tobacco pipe stem, in order that the water may dissolve as much as possible of the salt. When perfectly cold pour off the blue solution from the undissolved sulphate of copper (which should be reserved for future use), and add to it one-fourth of its bulk of the dilute sulphuric acid you use for exciting your plates. The acid is added in order to increase the power of the solution for conducting electrical currents, as it is a better conductor than either water or sulphate of copper solution Sulphate of copper, blue vitriol or blue stone, is generally met with in a pretty pure state. The solution it forms is sometimes cloudy at first, but subsidence and careful decantation easily remedy this evil.

We have now prepared our molds, zinc plates and solutions, and need only render the surface of the wax capable of conducting electricity to begin operations. This is effected by first gently wiping the wax impression with a tuft of cotton wool, to remove any dust or oil that may be on its surface, and then applying black lead to it with a soft plate brush until a black and brilliant gloss is produced. The brush should not be too hard, or the face of the mould will suffer; and the best black lead, bought at the instrument-maker's, should alone be used. The common quality, sold at the stores for domestic purposes, is quite useless, being generally adulterated with gritty matter. Black lead, or plumbago, was at one time supposed to be a compound of iron; but modern research has proved that it is non-metallic in its nature, being a peculiar form of carbon—the chemical name for pure charcoal. It may interest you to know that coke, lamp-black, charcoal, black lead, and diamond are only different forms of carbon. Plumbago, though not metal is an excellent conductor of electricity, and an electric telegram might be sent through a series of black lead pencils as easily as through an iron wire. The surface of the mold, therefore, when well brushed over with plumbago, becomes just as great a conductor of electricity as if it were gilt or silvered. You must be very careful to use sufficient black lead, so as to produce a continuous coating—indeed, it is hardly possible to use too much. The edges of the mould should be black-leaded about half way down, but the back, of course, is left in its natural condition.

Nothing now remains but to connect the mold with the battery and see the latter in action.

Supposing you are using a single-cell Daniell, pour the sulphate of copper solution into the outer jar until it reaches within an inch of the top, and place the porous cell in it. Pour the acid solution into the latter, taking care that the two solutions are level with each other, Next slightly warm the wire connected with the zinc, and insert it in the edge of the wax mould about half way between the back and front. When cool, make the electrical connection between the wire and the mould continuous by black-leading the point of the junction vigorously. Bend the wire into the shape of a long ∩, so that the face of the mould may be opposite the middle of the flat part of the zinc plate, and as near to it as possible. Immerse the zinc in the porous tube, and, if necessary, bring the mould nearer to it by bending the wire. The mould may possibly carry down with it a number of little bubbles of air, but these may be generally got rid of by tapping the wire with a key or knife. If they should resist this treatment, the mould must be moved up and down until they disappear; for if allowed to remain, you will find perfect copies of them on the surface of your electrotype. A little muslin bag of crystals of sulphate of copper should be hung just below the top of the copper solution so that the supply may be kept up.

If everything has gone right, metallic copper of a beautiful rose tint will gradually spread over the mould, beginning with the part in connection with the wire, and by degrees covering the whole of the black-leaded surfaces. The deposition does not begin immediately, but when once it commences, it goes on continuously as long as any is generated. The mould may be lifted out and the deposit examined with impunity, as long as it is not touched with the fingers. The amount of time necessary for the deposition varies with the size of the mould and the power of the battery, from twenty-four to forty-eight hours, or even longer. If the time is extended beyond twenty-four hours it is better, if the mould is large, to pour away the acid solution in the porous tube, and replenish it from stock.

Let me here say that every time you replenish the solution in the porous cell you should brush off the black fur that has formed upon the zinc, otherwise your battery will not work well.

When the deposit is sufficiently thick, the cast may be removed and another substituted for it. If you are careful you may remove the electrotype from the mould without injuring it; so that after being freshly black-leaded it may be used again.

If a Smee's battery is used, the copper solution is poured into a separate vessel. An ordinary jelly-jar answers the purpose. This separate vessel is termed the decomposing cell. The battery is excited with the dilute sulphuric acid as for the Daniell. You must take care that the ends of the screws and wires that come into contact are kept clean and bright, otherwise the current is greatly enfeebled. The battery being filled with the dilute acid, the wire from the zinc is attached to the mould as before. The wire from the silver is fastened to a piece of copper plate about twice the size of the mould to be covered. The two wires are then bent over so that the copper plate and mould may be exactly facing each other, and about an inch apart.

As the copper plate dissolves away, it must be replaced by a fresh one. You must also recollect that every grain of copper dissolved is reproduced on the mould; so that there is no necessity in having a bag of crystals in the solutions, as in the case of the Daniell arrangement.

The battery solution should be changed every forty-eight hours or so.

At first, no doubt, the young electrotyper will succeed in obtaining excellent results; but as he continues his experiments he will find that instead of getting a nice, even flexible coating of metallic copper, he will obtain either a crystalline, brittle deposit, or else a dirty brown powder forms on the surface of the mould. These failures occur from the electrical current being either too weak or too strong.

If all is not going well the best thing to do is to re-amalgamate the zinc plates and change the exciting solution. If these remedies do not have the desired effect we must examine the result and endeavor to discover in what particular we have failed.

I.—The copper deposit refuses to cover the whole of the mould;

This generally arises from there being a deficiency of black lead on the surface of the wax. The remedy is obviously to lift out the mould, wash it in clean water, dry it carefully with blotting paper, and black lead it afresh. There is, of course, no need to remove any of the copper that has already formed, as it will unite with the new deposit. It may as well be mentioned that this failure is one of the most common with beginners.

II.—The copper deposits in the form of a dark brown powder.

This is caused by the electrical current being too strong for the size of the mould. The remedy is manifestly to lessen the amount of electricity received by the mould which may be done In several ways:

(a) By pouring away some of the acid solution, and so lessening the surface of zinc acted upon.

(*b.*) By separating the mould and the zinc by a greater interval in the case of the Daniell, or by removing it to a greater distance from the copper plate, when using the Smee's arrangement. This has the effect of giving the electrical current a larger mass of liquid to traverse, causing some of it to be lost in the way.

(*c.*) By diminishing the size of the copper plate when using the Smee.

This cause of failure frequently happens when the reproduction of small seals are the object of our labors. The batteries described are sufficiently powerful to deposit copper on a mould as large as two inches square or even larger. Any mould smaller, will generally require the power of the battery to be diminished before a good result can be obtained; or, when the moulds are small, several may be attached to the same wire.

III.—The copper deposits in a brittle crystalline mass.

The remedies for this failure are so exactly the reverse of those to be applied in the second case that it would only be wasting valuable time to detail them. In cold weather the deposit sometimes becomes brittle from the action of the acid solution in the zinc being slightly diminished, the apparatus should therefore be kept at a little distance from the fire. This description of failure may also occur from the connecting wires not being clean and bright when they touch the binding screws, or from the screws not being screwed sufficiently tight.

You will see that I have given you examples of every kind of failure that can occur, with several remedies to be applied in each case.

The choice of these must be left to your own good judgment. One good rule to bear in mind is that the surface of the zinc acted upon should never be more than three, or at most four times that of the medal to be copied. If this rule is adhered to and the directions for preparing and renewing the solutions are complied with, there is really hardly a possibility of failure.

Having succeeded in obtaining a deposit of sufficient thickness, the copper impression is carefully removed from the mould, trimmed with a sharp pair of scissors and a fine cut file, and well washed with soap and water and a soft brush. It may then be cleaned with a little rotten-stone, or fine whiting made in.o a paste with water, a soft clean piece of chamois leather being used to give it a final polish.

The bright copper surface thus obtained is very beautiful, but it unfortunately soon becomes tarnished by exposure to the air, except, indeed, it be kept in an air tight case. It is advisable, therefore, to give it an artificial tarnish, so to speak, in order to allow it to be exposed with impunity. This is effected by th use of a bronzing liquid. Of these there are great numbers in use. One of the best is that recommended by Walker.

Boil for a quarter of an hour in an earthen pipkin a gill of good vinegar, one ounce of carbonate of ammonia, and an ounce of verdigris; the two last ingredients being reduced to powder previously. Then mix in a separate vessel, a drachm of sal-ammoniac and ten grains of oxalic acid in another gill of vinegar. When the sal-ammoniac and the oxalic acid are dissolved mix the two solutions and boil for five minutes. When cold, pour off the clear liquid and preserve in a well-corked bottle. It is used by being brushed well over the medal several times, the latter being heated over a lamp or candle between each application. The depth of color obtained by by this method is very fine.

Enough now has been said to enable the veriest tyro to carry on the electrotype process with success. If, after all, failure should be the result, it will be, I fear, the consequence of the lack of one of the following good qualities—patience, exactitude, judgment and perseverance.

NICKEL PLATING.

A WORD TO THOSE NOT FAMILIAR WITH THE ART OF NICKEL PLATING.—The same methods and agents are employed for depositing Gold, Silver, Copper and Nickel—each metal requiring a like solution and anode.

The deposition of the three first metals has already become one of the most important industries of the day; but Nickel having been a rare metal, of limited supply, its valuable qualities have been but little known by metal workers therefore its deposition has been practiced much less than the deposition of the other metals. But when it becomes generally known that Nickel is a brilliant, ductile and magnetic metal, that its tenacity is much greater than iron, is not tarnished by exposure to the air or moisture, and resists like gold or platinum, the attacks of sulphur and highly corrosive metallic solutions, withstands the action of heat resists wear and abrasion to a much greater degree than silver, and is of nearly the same color, it must necessarily become more extensively used for electro-plating than any of the other metals.

In answer to the many inquiries we have from those inexperienced, we would say that the preparations necessary to commence Nickel Plating are simple and inexpensive: With a small battery of two cells, an oblong wooden tank of size to suit the article to be plated, coated inside with asphalt and then filled with a nickel solution, nickel plates for anodes, and brass rods to suspend your plates and goods from, polishing and buffing lathes, with rouge and crocus, as well as vessels for an acid, an alkali, and a soft water bath for cleaning the work before putting it into the solution, which is required the same as in silver plating and one is fitted up to commence work.

In order to give the best results, it is necessary that the solution should be as nearly neutral as possible, and the double sulphate of nickel and ammonia is more generally preferred as being the most reliable and practical, giving a softer metal deposit and smoother surface which can be polished more readily than that obtained from other solutions. Dissolve ¾ lb. of the double sulphate of nickel and ammonia to each gallon of pure water, and the solution is ready for use. The specific gravity of the solution should be kept up to about six degrees of hydrometer.

When using a solution prepared with the double sulphate of nickel and ammonia, a solid, coherent, tenacious and flexible nickel can be deposited to any desired amount, thus rendering the electro-deposition of nickel practically valuable.

The metal deposited from the double sulphate of nickel and ammonia gives the full equivalent of metal for the electricity employed. If with this solution a battery power is used of an intensity of two groove cells, or thereabouts, a white deposit is obtained. The use of a battery of too high an intensity should be avoided. It is important that the depositing shall not be forced by the use of too strong a current.

The anode of the depositing cell should present a surface to the action of the solution somewhat larger than the surface upon which the deposit is being made—particularly in the double sulphate solution. The reason is that nickel dissolves so slowly that if the exposed surface is not larger than the surface on which the deposit is made, the solution will not keep saturated.

With pure solutions and sufficient anode surface, the deposition of nickel can be carried on continuuusly and as surely and certainly, as the deposition of copper from the common sulphate solutions.

Napier, in his Manual of Electro-metallurgy, speaks of nickel coating; that it is very easily deposited and may be prepared for this purpose by dissolving it in nitric acid, then adding cyanide of potassium to precipitate the metal, after which the precipitate is washed and dissolved by the addition of more cyanide of potassium. The cyanide of potash has proved unsuitable for nickel plating; he says that he has coated articles with nickel in 1847, and up to 1853, they still retained their brilliancy and continued untarnished. Napier gives also the following practical instructions for plating. It is indispensable that the battery should be so arranged that the quantity of electricity generated should correspond with the surface of the article to be coated, and that the intensity should bear reference to the state of the solution, that is to say, that the quantity should be sufficient to give the required coating of metal in a given time, and the intensity such as to cause the electricity to pass through the solution to the articles. It is also essential that the plates of metal forming the positive pole with the solution should be of corresponding surface to the articles to be coated, and face them on both sides. The main condition of nickel plating lies in these points: 1. To have the solution always kept neutral, it is necessary to test frequently the liquid by means of litmus paper, and if the same indicates a prevalence of acid, to add sufficient caustic ammonia to make the liquor perfectly neutral; also to replace occasionally the consumed salts: 2. To have the materials to be plated always clean, which if the goods are of iron, can be done by dipping them in a mixture of muriatic acid and water. The least scratch will prevent a complete coating.

THE CHLORIDE OF NICKEL AND AMMONIA is much used for plating, requiring but four ounces of salt to one gallon of water.

A SIMPLE NICKEL-PLATING APPARATUS, likewise in full operation, may also be described, as very satisfactory results are daily realized: 1. A bath or vat containing the usual nickel solution of double salt, three-quarter pounds to the gallon of hot water; five gallons is applied to the porous cell which contains the amalgamated zinc pole three inches broad, seven inches deep, and seven inches long, but touching within one-half inch all around from the cell. The copper wire is connected, to hold suspended the articles, such as faucets, pistols, or other ware to be plated with nickel; the operation goes on at once, and deposits the metallic nickel from its solutions in the space of three to four hours.

NAGEL'S PROCESS for electro-plating with nickel is based upon applying the double salts of sulphate of nickel and ammonia with the platinum positive pole. It consists in taking 400 parts of the sulphate of nickel and 200 parts of ammonia, dissolved in 6000 parts of hot water, and the ammonia of 0.900 spec. gravity, heated to one hundred degrees F.

Mr. Beardslee who is unquestionably the veteran in nickel-plating in the United States, says that ever since 1858 he has coated metals with electric currents; that he has found the chloride of nickel with a certain quantity of ammonia to be of great service.

He attributes any failures in depositing nickel to the following requirements.

1. Nickel must have a perfectly uniform and unchanging current of electricity; a Smee battery with a carbon negative plate, gives a powerful and constant current of electricity.

2. The nickel solutions with the chloride solutions may work better with acid instead of alkaline reaction; he quotes, as instances, that he had 2,000 gallons of nickel solutions since 1868 and '69, in constant use without any addition, but have been corrected from time to time in order to give them an acid reaction, as the tendency in working is to become alkaline.

He uses two cells of the Smee's battery; the amount of battery power required for a given amount of work to be done should be in zinc surface, equal to the surface to be coated.

The surface of the nickel anode should in no case be less than the surface to be coated. The anode surface for a nickel solution may be much greater than the surface to be coated, and more and better work will be the result.

For nickel solution of 40 gallons, 10 anodes of 6x12 inches are required, and in proportion to the greater or less quantity of gallons. By estimating 7½ gallons to each cubic foot, we can determine the amount of solution that will be required for a vat of any given size.

The nickel anodes are connected with the negative plate of the battery, which may be either the chromium or carbon plates; the articles to be coated are to be connected with the zinc pole of the battery.

In one gallon of nickel solution, a nickel anode of 4x6 inches is employed for coating small articles from two one gallon cells of the chromium negative plate battery.

SILVER PLATING.

The most important of all the arts of electro-deposition is that denominated "electro-plating." This beautiful art is now practiced to a vast extent in the United States, and Europe. Articles, chiefly made of German silver, are coated with fine silver, and thus, to a great extent, supersede the ordinary Sheffield and Birmingham plate; while old articles from which the silver has worn off can be replated, and thus rendered equal, and in some instances, superior to new.

Since the first introduction of the art, many have worked it with considerable success, and in the principal towns there are manufactories in which, annually, a vast amount of silver is deposited upon articles of various construction, and yet there is no superabundance of electro-platers; for I believe that if there were ten times the number, they would all do well, and for this reason:—the amount of plated goods now manufactured all over the world, far exceeds that made in the old days of Sheffield and Birmingham plate; and the silver which is deposited on these goods must be replaced as it wears off, in the progress of time, by the electro-plater. Again, many persons now use plated German silver goods in preference to silver, either owing to their superior beauty, their being less tempting to the marauder, or more economical to purchase. And when we bear in mind the vast quantity of electro-plate which is to be found in the hotels, restaurants, and private houses in the United States—which is daily having its silver rubbed and scrubbed off, there is good reason to believe that the electro-plater's services will be extensively required. in proportion as the manufacture and consumption of electro-plate progresses.

There are many solutions employed in depositing silver upon various metals, from which we will select those most likely to succeed with the beginner and the practical man. The proportions of the materials used being the same in small or large operations, the manipulator may easily make· up either of the following solutions in any quantity he pleases, from a pint to 1000 gallons or more.

SILVER SOLUTIONS.--In making any of these solutions, perfectly *fine* silver must be employed; or, if it is desired to use standard or other impure silver, it will be better to purify the silver by first dissolving it in nitric acid; then add about one quart of cold water to the acid solution obtained from dissolving four ounces of silver. Now throw in a few pieces of sheet cooper to precipitate the silver. When the pure silver is thus obtained, it is to be again dissolved in two parts water and one part nitric acid.

SOLUTION I.

```
Fine silver.......................................... 1 ounce.
Nitric acid.....................................about 1   „
Water.............................................. ½   „
```

Put the silver carefully into a Florence flask, and then pour in the acid and water; place the flask on a sand bath for a few minutes, taking care not to apply too much heat, and as soon as chemical action becomes violent, remove the flask to a cooler place, and allow the action to go on until it nearly ceases; when, if there be silver still undissolved, the flask may be again placed on the sand-bath until the silver disappears. If, however, the acid employed has been weak, it may be necessary to add a little more. The red fumes formed when chemical action is going on disappear when the silver is dissolved or when the acid has done its work. If a little black powder be visible at the bottom of the flask, it may be taken care of separately. as it is gold. I have frequently found gold in the silver purchased of a refiner; in some instances more than sufficient to pay the expense of the acid employed.

The nitrate of silver formed during the above operation should be carefully poured into a porcelain capsule, and heated until a pellicle appears on the surface, when it may be placed aside to crystallize. The uncrystallized liquor should then be poured from the crystals into another capsule, and heat applied until it has evaporated sufficiently to crystallize. When this is done, the crystals of nitrate of silver are to be placed in a large jar or other suitable vessel, and about three pints of cold distilled water added, the whole being well stirred with a glass rod until the crystals are dissolved.

A quantity of carbonate of potassa is now to be dissolved in distilled water, and some of the solution added to the nitrate of silver, until no further precipitation takes place. It is advisable occasionally to put a little of the clear solution in a glass, or test-tube, and to add a few drops of the solutiom of potassa, in order to ascertain whether all the silver is thrown down, or otherwise; as soon as the application of the alkaline solution produces no effect upon the solution of nitrate of silver, this operation is complete.

The supernatant liquor (that is, the fluid which remains above the precipitate) should next be carefully poured off the precipitated silver, and fresh water added; this is again allowed to settle, and the water poured off as before, which operation should be repeated several times in order to wash the precipitate thoroughly.

A quantity of cyanide of potassium is then to be dissolved in hot or cold water, and rather more than is sufficient to dissolve the precipitate added. In a few minutes the carbonate of silver will be dissolved by the cyanide, but in all probability there will be a trifling sediment at the bottom of the vessel, which may be separated from the solution by filtration, and preserved, as in all probability it will contain a little silver.

Sufficient water is now to be added to make one gallon of solution. Should the solution be found to work rather slowly at first, a little of the solution of cyanide may be added from time to time, as it is required; but it is preferable, in working a new solution, to have as small a proportion of cyanide as possible, otherwise the articles may *strip*, but more especially if they are composed of German silver.

When a silver solution has been worked for some length of time, it acquires organic matter, and is then capable of bearing, without injury, a larger proportion of cyanide.

It is necessary that the nitric acid employed for dissolving silver should be of good commercial quality, if not chemically pure, for if it contains hydrochloric acid (which is not an unfrequent adulteration), a portion of the silver dissolved will become precipitated in the form of a white flocculent powder (chloride of silver), and the success of the operation is thereby impaired.

SOLUTION II.—One ounce of fine silver treated as before, and dissolved in three pints of distilled water. Precipitate with common salt, and wash, as above directed. Dissolve the precipitate with a strong solution of cyanide of potassium, taking care not to add much more than will dissolve the chloride of silver. Filter carefully, at least once through the same filtering paper and once through clean filtering paper, and then add enough distilled water to make one gallon of solution.

The above solution is very useful when it is desired to plate an article delicately white, but the silver is liable to strip when the burnisher is applied to it. This solution, however, may be employed with less fear of the work stripping, if it be used weaker, with a small surface of anode and feeble battery power.

Under all circumstances this solution is more applicable to surfaces which only require to be scratch-brushed, or which are to be left *dead.* Chased figures, clock-dials, cast metal work, etc., may be admirably plated with this solution.

SOLUTION III   Dissolve in one gallon of water one ounce and a-quarter of cyanide of potassium, in a stone-ware or glass vessel. Filled a porous cell with some of this solution, and place it in the larger vessel; the solution should be the same height in both vessels.   Then put a piece of sheet copper or iron, connected with the wire which proceeds from the zinc of the battery, into the porous cell.   Place in the stone vessel a piece of stout sheet silver, which must be previously attached to the wire issuing from the copper of the battery.   It is well to employ several cells alternated, for this purpose, when a large quantity of solution has to be prepared; that is to say, the zinc of one battery should be united by a wire with the copper of the next, and so on.   In a few hours the solution in the larger vessel will have acquired sufficient silver, and the solution may be at once used.   The porous cell is to be removed, and its contents may be thrown away.

In working this solution at first it is necessary to expose a rather large surface of anode, and small quantities of cyanide must be added occasionally until the solution is in brisk working order.

This is one of the best solutions, when carefully prepared, and is less liable to strip than many others.

When it is desired that the articles should come out of the bath having a *bright* appearance, a little bisulphuret of carbon is added to the solution.   This is best done in the following manner:—Put an ounce of bisulphuret of carbon into a pint bottle containing a strong silver solution with cyanide in excess.   The bottle should be repeatedly shaken, and the mixture is ready for use in a few days.   A few drops of this solution may be poured into the plating bath occasionally, until the work appears sufficiently bright.   The bisulphuret solution, however, must be added with care, for an excess is apt to spoil the solution.   In plating surfaces which cannot easily be scratch-brushed, this brightening process is very serviceable.   The operator, however, must never add too much at a time.

In making up the foregoing solutions the weights and measures epmloyed are troy or apothecaries' weight, and imperial measure.

Having at command any of the solutions described, the operator may next arrange the battery.   A plate *a, a, a,* or sheet of silver, is to be attached to the wire issuing from the copper of the battery *b,* and supported by a brass rod *d :* this may be done either by soldering them together or uniting them with a suitable binding screw; but the best plan of attaching the anode, or sheet of silver, to the copper wire is as follows:—Cut a strip to within

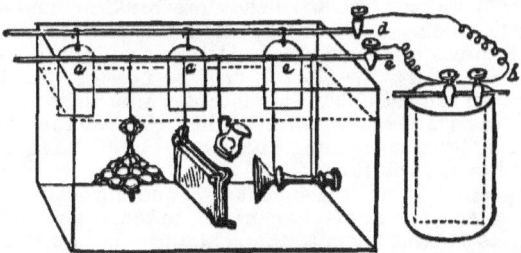

half an inch or so; this strip may be united to the wire by a binding screw or soldered. If cast plates of silver are used, it is advantageous to have them cast with an extra piece, about three inches long at the corners, to attach the copper wire to.

The object in adopting either of the above arrangements is to prevent the copper wire entering the bath, as this is much impaired by allowing the copper to be immersed in the cyanide solution, whether deposition is taking place or not. Copper, if left in the bath for any length of time, even unconnected with a battery, will reduce a portion of the silver from the solution, an equivalent of the copper taking its place. This is especially the case when a large quantity of free cyanide is present.

A brass rod e, with a binding screw soldered or screwed on one end of it, is now attached to the negative wire of the battery. The articles to be coated may be suspended to this rod by pieces of clean copper wire; the wire used for this purpose may be rather thin, yet sufficiently strong to bear the weight of the articles. The thinner the wire is the less mark will be made upon the articles coated—a very important consileration in some cases, especially where spoons and forks are to be plated. This wire is termed "slinging wire." The size I generally prefer for spoons and forks is about 1-32d of an inch in thickness. The rods from which the anodes and goods to be plated are suspended must be kept quite clean and bright by rubbing with emery cloth.

Spoons may be well brushed with either powdered pumicestone or powdered bath-brick (I prefer the latter) and water—a hard brush being applied to the purpose. This cleausing process is carried on until all the polish of the spoons is removed; and the fingers which hold the articles should be kept well charged with the powdered material, to prevent any grease or perspiration being imparted to the work. In cleaning spoons it is advisable to begin at the inside of the bowl, and then to proceed to the other parts; lastly, going over the whole surface lightly, to render it uniform after the necessary handling it has been subject to. A little practice will soon render the operator expert in these important details. The spoons, etc., are to be placed in clean cold water as soon as they are brushed, and are then ready for the bath. The slinging wires may now be attached

When a solution is newly made, the work is apt to be irregularly coated at first, therefore it may be necessary to take the articles out of the bath about ten minutes after their first immersion, and to give them another slight rub with the brush and powdered material as before, when they should be again rinsed and placed in the solution.

If it is desired to give the spoons a very strong coating of silver, it is well, after a few hours' immersion, to remove them from the bath, and to submit them to the action of a lathe scratch-brush (consisting of a "chuck," with several bundles of fine brass wire attached to it, upon which beer or weak ale is allowed to run from a small barrel, with a tap to it, from above). This process will burnish down the white "burr," as it is called, and which consists of minute crystals of fine silver, and will prevent the coating from becoming *rough*. After the articles are scratched they should be rinsed in clean water, and again placed in the bath until done. The spoons may be lightly brushed over with moistened silver sand instead of being scratch-brushed, but the latter is preferable. When the goods have received the required coating they are again scratched, and can then be finished, either by the burnisher or polisher.

ELECTRO-DEPOSITION OF GOLD.

In importance, electro-gilding is second only to the art of electro-plating; and it is carried on in much the same way. The solutions of gold, however, must be worked *hot*; hence the operation of gilding is conducted in a much shorter space of time than is required for plating. An article may be well and strongly coated in a few minutes, while it would require several hours to electro-plate an article well.

There are many forms of solution in use amongst electro-metallurgists, all of them varying in the proportion of gold to the gallon of water, and in the amount of cyanide employed. These solutions are all of them easily made, and any of them can be well worked by a skilful operator. Some gilders use five or six pennyweights of gold to the quart of solution—others as much as eight or ten dwts.; but I have generally found that a solution containing less gold will give better results than one richer in the metal, independent of the advantage of economy. I have observed that a bath containing five or six dwts. of gold to the quart of water, and the necessary proportion of cyanide, and worked with several united cells of Smee's battery, has required a much larger surface of anode to be exposed to a given surface of negative electrode (that is, the article to be gilt) than would be required to gild an article in a solution containing one and a half dwt. to the quart of solution worked with a single cell of a constant battery. Hence I infer that the weaker solution, is the better conductor of the two.

GOLD SOLUTINS.—SOLUTION I.—Dissolve in a Florence flask one pennyweight and a half of fine gold in two parts hydrochloric acid and one part nitric acid (*aqua regia*,) applying gentle heat to accelerate chemical action. When the the gold is all dissolved, pour the chloride of gold thus formed into a porcelain capsule and apply moderate heat until all the acid is evaporated. A red mass will result. It is advisable, when the acid is nearly expelled, to move the capsule round and round, so that the liquid may be dispersed over a large surface of the vessel. It will be found that the liquid will cease to flow when the acid is expelled, at which period the operation is complete. If too much heat is applied the gold will become reduced to the metallic state, which may be known by the red mass acquiring first a yellow tinge, and next a gold bronze will be observed at the bottom of the capsule. In such a case it will be necessary to add a little more of the mixed acids in the same proportion as before, which will at once re-dissolve the reduced gold.

When the acid has been driven off the chloride of gold, about half a pint of cold distilled water is to be added, which will at once dissolve the chloride, forming a bright straw-colored solution. Allow this to subside for a few minutes, as in all probability there will be a small amount of white percipitate at the bottom of the vessel, which is chloride of silver ; the solution of gold must be carefully poured off from this precipitate, as it is soluble in cyanide of potassium, and its presence in the resulting solution may be prejudicial. A little distilled water may be poured into the capsule, to rinse away all the gold, taking care not to allow the sediment to come away with it, when transferring the rinsings to the solution of gold.

A little stong solution of cyanide is now added, gradually, to the solution of gold, and the whole stirred with a glass rod. The gold solution will instantly lose its yellow color. A brown precipiate is formed by the solution of cyanide, and this must be added drop by drop until it produces no further effect upon the clear solution. The supernatant liquor is now to be carefully poured off and fresh water added several times to wash the percipitate of gold—taking care not to waste any of the precipitate nor to add more cyanide than is absolutely necessary. When the precipitate is sufficiently washed, more of the solution of cyanide is added, which will at once dissolve the precipitate, forming a clear solution. The cyanide should be added in excess, say about twice as much as may be required to dissolve the precipitate. The concentrated solution of cyanide of gold thus obtained is placed over the fire or on a sand-bath until it is evaporated to dryness, when it may be again dissolved in cold water and filtered for use. Lastly, enough boiling distilled water is added to make one quart of solution, and a little additional cyanide added if the solution is found to work too slowly at first but it is better not to use more cyanide than is necessary, otherwise the anode will become rapidly consumed and the gilding be of a "foxy" color.

SOLUTION II. Dissolve one and a half dwt., fine gold as before, and evaporate to dryness. Re-dissolve in half a pint of distilled water and precipitate the gold with ammonia, taking care not to add more ammonia than is necessary. Pour off the supernatant liquor and wash the precipitate as before. Now add sufficient cyanide of potassium to dissolve the precipitate. Evaporate to dryness, and re-dissolve with cold distilled water. The solution is then to be filtered, and distilled water added to make one quart. A little cyanide is to be added occasionally, as required.

SOLUTION III. Dissolve one dwt. and a half as before, and when the half pint of solution of chloride is obtained, precipitate the gold with hydrosulphate of ammonia. A copious black precipitate is formed, which must be allowed to subside, and this substance then washed as before directed. Dissolve the precipitate with a lump of cyanide—say about half an ounce, or rather less; and evaporate to dryness. Then add water to make one quart.

SOLUTION IV. Dissolve the same quantity of gold as before, but without evaporating the acid. Add a quantity of calcined magnesia, which will precipitate the gold in the form of an oxide. To the oxide add sufficient concentrated nitric acid (applying heat at the same time) to dissolve the magnesia, when the oxide will be left in the form of a precipitate, which is to be well washed, and then solution of cyanide added to dissolve it as before. Evaporate and make one quart of solution with distilled water.

These solutions should be worked at a temperature of about 130 deg. F., with one cell of a constant battery.

The solution of gold may be heated either in an enameled saucepan, or in a glass vessel placed in an iron pan containing water. The operator now proceeds to arrange his battery. The wire which issues from the copper of the battery is to be attached to a piece of fine gold, which may conveniently be done by soldering. The article to be gilt is to be suspended to the wire proceeding from the zinc of the battery.

PREPARATION OF ARTICLES TO BE GILT.—Silver goods, such as cream ewers, sugar bowls, mugs, etc., should be well scoured inside with hot soap and water and silver sand, and if they are at all greasy, a little caustic soda may be applied to them first.

Or the mugs, etc., may be well scratch-brushed and then rinsed with boiling water. The insides only of these vessels are generally required to be gilt, in which case the outsides may be wiped dry before gilding. The negative wire (from the zinc of the battery) is to be attached to the handle of the vessel. The plate of gold is now to be carefully suspended in the centre of the mug, taking care that it does not touch the vessel; and the gold solution may be poured into the mug by means of a jug or other suitable vessel, until it reaches the upper edge.

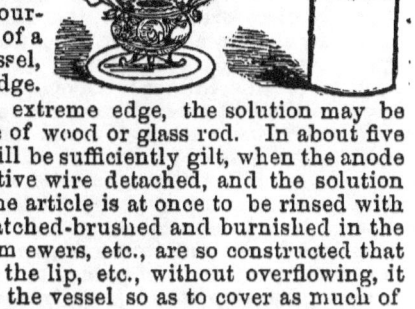

If it is desired to gild the extreme edge, the solution may be guided over it with a piece of wood or glass rod. In about five or six minutes the vessel will be sufficiently gilt, when the anode may be removed, the negative wire detached, and the solution poured into the bath. The article is at once to be rinsed with hot water, and may be scratched-brushed and burnished in the ordinary way. When cream ewers, etc., are so constructed that the solution will not reach the lip, etc., without overflowing, it is advisable to slightly tilt the vessel so as to cover as much of it as possible, and when it is gilt the lip may be dipped into a little gold solution, being attached to the battery the while; but in this case the outside of the lip will also receive a deposit. This may be prevented by coating the outer surface of the vessel with melted gutta-percha, Vessels which are to be gilt inside only, should be placed on a plate or dish to collect any solution which may run over.

Silver brooches, pins, rings, thimbles, egg, salt and mustard spoons, etc., merely require to be scratched-brushed before gilding. After they have received the required deposit, they are again brushed, and if the color be a little too pale or too red, the articles should be immersed in the bath again *for an instant*, and then plunged into boiling water, when they will assume a beautiful fine gold color. When well rinsed in hot water, the articles are to placed in a box of saw-dust, which may sometimes be advantageously kept hot for this purpose, in order to dry the goods as speedily as possible; but care must be taken that the box-dust be not allowed to char or burn, otherwise it will stain the articles.

Goods which are made of copper or brass entirely may be dipped into nitrous acid ("fuming nitric acid" or "dipping acid") for a moment, and instantly plunged into clean cold water; after which process they should be again rinsed in fresh water, and at once placed in the gilding bath. Or, such articles may be merely scratched-brushed, rinsed, and then placed in the bath.

A NEW SOURCE OF ELECTRICITY, OR ELECTRIC-

ITY PRODUCED BY MOTION.

We now come to a new, and, for large establishments, more economical process of generating electrical currents, which is destined to supersede all the before mentioned hydro-electric batteries, for the deposition of metals on a large scale.

Faraday discovered in 1831, that the establishment and cessation of an electric current in a conductor, induced similar currents in any conductor running paralled to the same. The direction of this induced current, is reverse to the primary current in the first case, alike in the second case. Shortly after it was found that a magnet would' act in the same manner as a conductor traversed by a current. Pixu was the first who constructed a machine utilizing this discovery of magneto-induction, which was soon improved by Saxton, Clark, and V. Ettingshausen. In all these machines helices of insulated copper wire were slipped over soft iron cores, and brought alternately under the inductive influence of permanent magnets. Siemens made the next great step in advance, by giving the iron core in the induction coil, that peculiar form which is known all over the world, as the Siemens armature. It resembles a long cylinder, into which two deep and wide grooves are cut on opposite sides parallel to its axis. Into these grooves the wire is coiled, also parallel to the axis. This armature revolves between the poles of a number of permanent magnets, and gives a powerful current for the weight of material employed. It soon occured to Wild, that this current could be used to excite an electro-magnet of great power, which in turn would induce currents in a large Siemens armature revolved between its poles. The machines constructed by him on that principle, gave astonishing results, and were fit for many industrial purposes. They are even now used to a great extent.

Wheatstone and Siemens, found that the charging machine could be dispensed with, as the current from the armature could be taken through the coils of the electro-magnet to excite the same, the machine starting with the small residuum of magnetism which every electro-magnet retains, after being once charged Since then a great many machines have been constructed differing in shape, and more or less complicated; but all making use of the principle of magneto-induction.

The conversion of the motive power driving these machines into electricity, is accomplished with more or less loss. Some makers claim to utilize 75 per cent, but such high results appear doubtful. But in any case the magneto-electric machine is a great economizer, as it consumes nothing but the motive power and some lubricating oil for its journals, while the hydro electric batteries consume zinc, acids, mercury, and the attendants time for cleaning and amalgamating. Besides the current is uniform if the speed is regular and no unhealthy fumes are developed, All large establishments for electro-deposition, are availing themselves already of the advantages which these machines give over the ordinary batteries.

As the passage of an electric current through a conductor is heating, the same, in proportion to the resistance which this conductor offers, it was soon found necessary to devise means for cooling the coils of dynamo electric machines, to prevent the charring and ultimate destruction of the insulating material. There is also heat developed by the rapid pole changing which the cores of the induction coils have to undergo.

Wild, passed water through hollow brass pieces, which were interposed between the poles of the magnet, leaving a cylindrical space in which the armature revolved. Another maker cast the pole ends of the magnet hollow, and passed water through them. The armature has also been pierced from end to end, and a stream of water run through. The most effective plan for cooling, has been lately devised by W. Hochausen, who makes the magnetic field a water-tight compartment, in which the armature revolves, in thorough contact with the water, keeping thereby both the iron core and the coil perfectly cold.

PRICE LIST

OF

GOLD, SILVER & NICKLE PLATING

AND

COPPER BRONZING SUPPLIES

(Prices subject to variation without notice.)

These prices are remarkably low, as will be seen by comparing them with those of other manufacturers.

No. 1.—The Single-Cell Electroplating Battery.

PRICE $1.50.

This battery is a marvel of cheapness and utility combined.

With one of these batteries all the cuts in this book have been electrotyped, which will show practically what the batteries are capable of doing.

This apparatus consists of a flint glass jar 4 by 4 inches, into which a porous cup and a square of zinc with a wire attached to one end for hanging the objects to, is placed in the porous cup.

The battery is charged by dissolving sulphate of copper in hot water, and adding about a half ounce of sulphuric acid to the solution, so as to increase its conducting power. Take the balance of the sulphate of copper and put it in a bag and hang it on the side of the glass, as shown in the engraving. Place the porous cup in the glass a little to one side, with the zinc in it; fill the porous cup up with water; then add a few drops of sulphuric acid, and the battery will be ready for use.

1

Hang the article to be plated on the brass wire so that it will be covered by the solution in the glass, and the copper will be immediately deposited.

This battery will be sent to any address, packed in a neat box, with some sulphate of copper, wire, and book of instructions, for $1.25.

No. 2 Battery, single cell, packed in a neat box, but with a quarter of a pound of the best prepared wax for taking impressions, one ounce of the best plumbago, and one soft brush—in fact, everything that is necessary to set to work and copper casts of coins, medals, &c., complete, with book of instructions, sent to any address for **$2.25.**

SMEE PLATING BATTERY.

The single-cell battery is not often used when there is a large amount of work to be done, as it is not so handy as the Smee, or other forms of batteries.

Smee's Electroplating Battery when in Use.

For deposition of Gold, Silver, Nickle, Copper, and other metals.

PRICE $3.00.

This is the smallest kind of Smee battery that we make. It has two zinc plates two and three quarters by three and a half inches, carbon centre, two brass binding-posts, as shown in the engraving. With this battery is given a white annealed flint glass jar, four by four inches, for holding the solution, two brass rods for connecting the battery wire. To one end of these rods is connected a piece of sheet copper, the other is used to suspend the article to be plated. Sufficient sulphate of copper to make a saturated solution and book of instructions, all packed in a neat box, and sent to any address for $3. This is cheapest plating apparatus made.

2

No. 4 Battery, the same as the above, but with the addition of a quarter pound of the best prepared wax, one ounce best plumbago, one soft brush, packed in a neat box, for $4.25.

No. 5 Battery, the same as the above, but with one quart of silver solution, one piece of sheet silver, and one hard brush,— substituted for the plumbago, wax, and soft brush,— packed in a neat box, for $5.00.

Sample Shells, showing the work of these batteries, in copper, sent to any address for twenty cents.

Besides the above we manufacture larger sizes of Smee's battery, and other forms for manufacturing purposes.

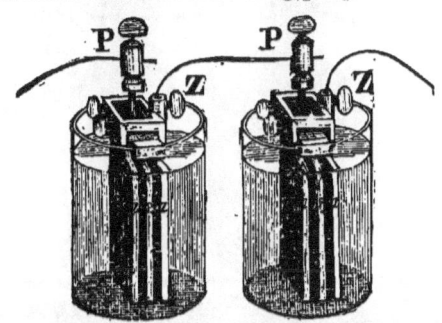

No. 6 Battery, Smee battery, zinc plates, $4\frac{3}{4}$x$3\frac{1}{2}$ inches wide, in white annealed glass jars, for $3.00.

No. 7 Battery, Smee battery, zinc plates, 4x8 inches, in white annealed glass jars, for $5.00.

No. 8 Battery, Smee battery zinc plates, $7\frac{1}{2}$x$11\frac{1}{2}$ inches, in stone jars, carbon centre, for $12.00.

Any of the parts of the above batteries, will be sold separately when wanted.

No. 9, Lowey's Jewelers' Plating Battery, $20.00. $25.00.

The Batteries are composed of glass or porcelain jars, holding about two quarts of solution. P represents the positive poles, and Z the negative poles of the battery. Z Z are the two zinc plates, and P is the carbon plate of the battery. B is an iron stand, for the purpose of holding the Gilding or Silvering Pan containing the plating solution. F is two bars of brass or copper to connect the poles of the batteries to, and also to hang on the articles to be plated.

T is a thermometer, which is used to ascertain the temperature of the solution. The gilding solution requires to be about 110 degrees. Silver solution is worked cold.

3

Set complete, consisting of two two-quart Smee' Batteries, in cluding Gilding Pan, Brass Bars, Spirit Lamp, and Thermoneter, Price $20.00. Same with two extra Batteries, thus giving greatly augmented power and facilities, $25.

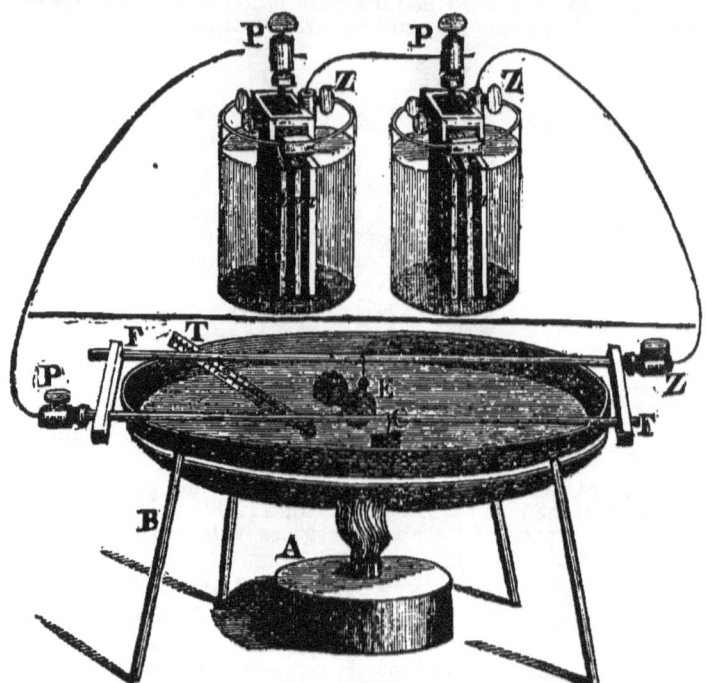

W. LOWEY'S Improved Batteries, connected.
With Gilding Pan in the act of gilding a Watch-Case.

BUNSEN BATTERIES.

These batteries are used whenever a very intense current is needed, as in plating Iron, Steel, Britannia Metal, etc. It is the battery that is now most generally used by the nickel platers of this city.

Of this battery we have three sizes:—

No. 10 consists of a white annealed flint-glass jar holding about one quart, a zinc with a porous cup fitting in the centre, and carbon with platinum connection, for $2.50.

4

No. 11 glass holding two quarts, and other parts in propor tion, for $3.50.

No. 12 glass holding one gallon, with rolled zinc, $5.50.

These batteries are very intense, and where a strong current is needed, as in coating Iron, Steel, and Britannia Metal, is the one generally employed. It is this battery we are now. supplying to the nickel-platers in this city and vicinity.

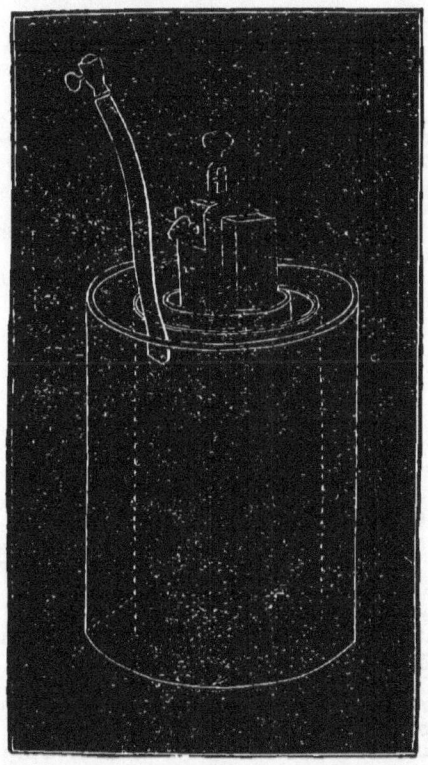

No. 8 and 9 are a very convenient size, as they take up but little room. The glass jar is the size of a large quart tumbler. We generally sell two cells for plating. (No. 8) They will answer for fixing the solutions and finishing. They will plate iron, steel, and Britannia. I have nsed them on all these metals so difficult to plate. It is very intense, and drives the silver on very rapidly.

5

PARTS OF BATTERIES.

Any of the parts of these batteries will be supplied separately when so ordered, such as—

Glasses holding one quart, 50 cents; two quarts, 75 cents; one gallon, $1.25.

Porous cups, for No. 1, 25 cents; No. 2, 50 cents; No. 3, 75 cents.

Carbons for the small batteries,—the smallest $3\frac{1}{2}$x$2\frac{1}{2}$, 80 cents; size 4x3, $1.00; size $5\frac{1}{2}$x$4\frac{1}{2}$, $2.00; size $11\frac{1}{2}$x$7\frac{1}{2}$, $4.25; 6x9, $3.50.

Carbons for the Bunsen batteries—No. 1, 50 cents; No. 2, 75 cents; No. 3, $1.50.

Brass Clamps for the Smee batteries—battery 3x3, 50 cents; larger sizes, $1.00.

Binding-Posts, small batteries, 25 cents; large, 50 cents.

Connecting-Bars, with binding-posts on the end for connecting the battery wires, each 75 cents.

Zinc of all kinds, for both Smee and Bunsen batteries. Rolled zinc cut to any pattern.

We also put up sets of apparatus to meet the wants of certain classes of people in business at very low figures.

SILVER-PLATER'S SET.

If persons, in ordering, do not want all the articles enumerated in the following sets, they can select whatever they may require, which, of course, will make the set cost less.

4 two-quart batteries, connections, stand, pan, thermometer, etc.
4 pints of silver solution.
1 bottle of cyanide of copper.
1 bottle of nitrate of mercury.
1 bottle of cyanide of potassa.
1 graduated glass.
1 bottle of crocus.
1 bottle of rouge.
Glass sticks and wires.
1 box of sawdust.
Sawdust brush.
2 brushes.
2 scratch-brushes.

2 decomposing dishes.
1 box pumice stone.
1 box of whiting.
1 bottle bright mixture, for bright plating.
1 plate of silver.
1 copper.
3 connecting-cups.
1 pound of mercury
2 burnishers.
1 brass blowpipe.
1 lamp.
1 bottle gold solution.
24 filtering papers.

These articles are all packed in a box, with book of instructions on plating in gold and silver. Price, **$40.**

6

JEWELERS' SET.

In this set is included all that is necessary for a Jeweler or Watch-Repairer to start in buiness with. It comprises all the Batteries, Solutions, Chemicals, and Apparatus that are required, with Instructions, viz. :

2 two-quart Smee's Batteries.	1 soft brush for cleaning work.
2 " Solution Dishes.	1 box of ground pumice stone.
1 stand, with pan.	1 " whiting.
1 pint of cyanide of silver, with bottle.	2 connecting cups.
	1 graduated glass.
½ pound of cyanide of potassa, with bottle.	2 glass rods, for stirring solutions.
1 bottle of nitric acid, with ground stopple,	1 hand brush.
Mercury and bottle,	1 burnisher.
Silver plate and wire.	1 bottle of crocus.
Gold plate and wire.	1 piece of chamois. leather.
1 scratch-brush.	1 bottle rouge.
1 lamp.	1 blowpipe.
	1 box and thermometer.

These articles are all packed in a box, with Instructions, and can be sent by express to any part of the world perfectly safe.

Price $ 32.00.

SET FOR TRAVELLING PLATERS.

2 Bunsen batteries.	1 graduate glass.
1 extra glass cup.	1 scratch brush.
2 " porous cups.	1 sand brush
2 rods, 24 inches with cups.	1 fine brush.
2 12-ft. conducting wires.	1 burnisher.
1 book of instructions.	1 lb. hanging wire.
1 glass funnel.	1 box pumice stone.
½ pound quicksilver.	1 box whiting.
1 magnet.	1 box of rouge.
1 pair of scales.	1 box of crocus.

This set will be packed and sent to any address on receipt of

Price $18.00.

BLOODSTONE BURNISHERS.

Eleven sizes. Prices from $ 1.25. to $ 11.00.

ANODES.

Prices subject to variation, and will be furnished on application.
Gold and silver anodes rolled in any required shape. Granulated gold and silver for making solutions.

Pure nickel anodes, 2¼x6 inches....................
"   "   "   2¼x9   "   ....
"   "   "   4x10   "   ....
              Any other sizes to order.
Pure nickel in grains................................
Single salts of nickel and ammonia..................
Double "   "   "   ....
Chloride of   "   "   ....
Copper anodes of all sizes..........................

SOLUTIONS.

Solutions of all kinds on hand and made to order.
Gold solution containing 2½ dwt. to the quart..........
Silver, solution containing four ounces to the gallon,
     per gallon.....................................
Cyanide of copper, per quart.......................
"   "   " gallon.......................
Lowey's Hydrometer for testing the strength of solutions

STEEL BURNISHERS.

Swiss Oval Steel, two sizes, 60 cents each.
French Oval Steel, in handles, curved and straight ends, 75 cents
     each.
French Agate, in handles, $1.30. each.
Stubbs' steel, in handles, three sizes, from 50 to 75 cents each.
Steel Burnishers, of any required pattern, made to order, at prices
     varying according to size and shape.
Casseroles, or Coloring Pots, from 3 to 6½ inches in diameter 75
     cents to $3.00

POLISHING POWDERS.

Emery first quality, 25 cents per pound.
Emery Cloth of the best brands, 15 cents per sheet, $1.50 per
     quire.
Emery Paper, American, best quality, all sizes 5 cents per sheet,
     75 cents per quire.
French Emery Paper, first quality, 5 cents per sheet, 40 cents
     per dozen.

Pumice Stone, powdered 20 cents per lb.
"   "   lumps, 15 cents per lb.

ROUGE.

Crocus, 75 cents per pound.
Rouge, hard, second quality, $1 per pound.
"   "   first quality, $1.25 per pound.
"   soft, in balls, $1.25 per pound.

BRUSHES.

Wooden handles, first quality, 3 rows, 30 cents; 4 rows, 35 cents;
    5 rows, 40 cents; 6 rows, 45 cents.
Wooden handles, extra quality, 3 rows, 35 cents, 4 rows, 40 cents;
    5 rows, 45 cents; 6 rows, 55 cents.
Wooden handles, goat hair, 3 rows, 40 cents; 4 rows 50 cents.

BRASS SCRATCH-BRUSHES.

Prices from 60 cents to $3.00, according to size.

STEEL SCRATCH-BRUSHES.

Prices from 40 cents to $2.50, according to size.

BRASS END-BRUSHES.

Large, $1.00; small, 75 cents.

BRASS SCRATCH WHEEL-BRUSHES.

	2 rows.	3 rows.
2 inches diameter, each	$1.50	$1.75
3 " " "	2.00	2.75
4 " " "	2.75	3.75

HAND BUFFS.

LEATHER.

Plain, per dozen, 75 cents. each 7 cents.
Heavy, per dozen, $1.25; each, 12 cents.
Half round, per dozen, $1.00; each, 10 cents.
Round, per dozen, $1.25; each, 12 cents.

FELT.

Plain, per dozen, $2.50; each, 25 cents.
Heavy, per dozen, $2.50; each, 25 cents.
Round, per dozen, $3.50; each, 35 cents.
Round buffs, all sizes and thicknesses, to order.

Polishing and Buffing Machinery.

All of this machinery is made in the best manner, with steel spindles and hard metal bearings, and is designed for quick speeds with cloth and brush wheels. Walrus leather and leather covered wheels. These machines have proved by long use to be the best in the market.

No. 1.—JEWELERS' POLISHING LATHE.

This lathe as shown in the cut stands seven and three - quarters inches high, and has a spindle seventeen and a half inches long by three-quarters of an inch diameter. The screw on the spindle is accurately turned and is fine enough to use with the smallest

Price $15.

brush. The spindle between the collars is seven and one-sixteenth of an inch diameter. They are also made one end with taper screw, the other end bored taper to receive ring buffs, with thread outside to screw on buff chucks. They are made with a V pulley, and also with tight and loose pulleys. Tight and loose pulleys will be sent unless otherwise ordered.

No. 2.—LIGHT BUFFING LATHE.

Price $25.

These lathes stand twelve inches high and have spindles two feet nine inches long, one and one-quarter inches diameter and weighs forty-nine pounds. They are made with collars on each end of the spindle, one collar and one screw, and two screws, also with fast and loose pulleys, and with one wide fast pulley. The spindles between the collars is three-quarters of an inch in diameter. Unless otherwise stated, orders will be filled with tight and loose pulleys and with one collar and one screw, as shown in the cut.

No. 3.—JEWELERS' DOUBLE SPEED POLISHING LATHE.

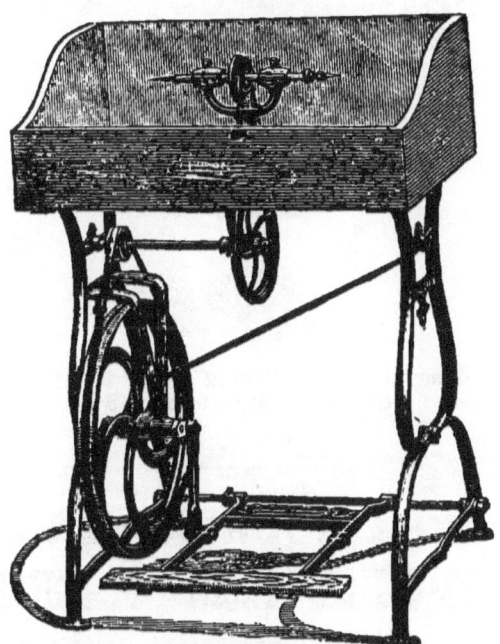

Price $75.

These lathes have been designed to supply a long felt want, where economy of space and good workmanship were desirable in a foot power lathe. By means of the patent V belt we have been able to place a countershaft under the table, which can only be done successfully by means of this belt. The pulleys on the countershaft are arranged to give about twenty-seven revolutions of the lathe spindle to one revolution of the crank which at fifty strokes a minute, give a speed of 1,350 revolutions, a speed which makes it especially desirable for extra fine polishing, scratch-brushing and satin finishing. The lathe stands seven and three-quarter inches high and has a spindle seventeen and a half inches long, by three-quarters of an inch diameter. The screw on the spindle is accurately turned and is fine enough to use with the smallest brush. The spindle between the collars is seven-sixteenths of an inch in diameter. They are also made one end with the taper screw, the other end bored toper to receive ring buffs, with thread outside to screw on buff chucks. The table of this machine is made of black walnut, twenty inches by thirty-four inches, with two drawers, and is zinc lined. The frame is of iron and is well braced, and has a strong jointed treadle and turned pulleys. The connecting rod has brass bearings.

We also sell small cheap polishing lathes $6, $7 and $8, and Balance wheels for foot power $8, $10 and $15 each.

THE HOCHHAUSEN
DYNAMO-ELECTRIC MACHINES,

For Electrotyping, Silver, Nickel, Brass, Copper-Plating and Gilding.

DESCRIPTION OF THE MACHINES.

A Siemens armature of improved shape rotates between the curved ends of a magnet, composed of two iron plates. A copper conductor is wound round each core of the magnet, and another from end to end into the armature groove. The two ends from the latter coil are attached to the insulated, lengthwise divided halves of a metal cylinder, from which the electricity induced is taken up by two collectors, made of flexible sheet-copper, which press against this cylinder at opposite sides. The

12

Nos. 1 and 2 machines have a countershaft fixed to their stands below the magnet, which carries fast and loose pulleys and a cone pulley to drive the armature. In the No. 3 machine the countershaft is best fixed overhead. It is not included in the price, as it is with Nos. 1 and 2, but will be made to order.

This machine works on the dynamo electric principle. The magnet holds some feeble residual magnetism which is imparted to it by passing a current of electricity through its coils, or by holding a magnet to it, pole to pole. This feeble magnetism, which always remains, induces a weak current in the armature coil when the latter is turned, but as this current is allowed to circulate through the coils of the magnet it strengthens the same, and this increased magnetic power will in turn induce currents in the armature coil of augmented force. The reciprocal action between armature and magnet produces a maximum of current after a few turns. This maximum is evidently greater for a high speed than for a moderate one. Setting the machine up to electroplate with, the anode and cathode rods on tank, and the galavnometer and resistance wires on switchboard are placed in circuit by good copper conductors, as shown in cut. Let the armature of No. 1 revolve 1,200, No. 2 1,000, No. 3, 900 times per minute. The machines for electrotyping purposes differ in electromotive force from those for the deposition of silver, nickel, brass, gold and copper from a Cyanide solution. The former represent strong single cells of very large surface, the latter a number of smaller cells connected in series. As the relative proportion between the anode and cathode surface varies considerably in working the metals mentioned, the current must be governed accordingly. This is accomplished by increasing or diminishing the length, and consequently the resistance of a wire, by a switch fastened to a board which also carries a galvanometer indicating the amount of current passing. This instrument is furnished with all machines except those for electrotyping where it is not needed, as the anode is always kept proportionate to the cathode.

The switch is arranged in such a manner that the circuit is completely open when the lever is pushed to the left as far as it will go. By moving it to the next contact plate to the right, the circuit is closed, but the current has to traverse the whole of the resistance wire, and is consequently feeble. Moving the lever still farther to the right, cuts out a part of this wire, decreasing thereby the resistance and increasing the strength of the current. This action of diminishing the resistance and augmenting the strength of the current goes on as the leaver is moved more and more to the right, till, coming to the end of its field of action, the whole of the resistance wire is cut out and the current is at its maximum for the amount of cathode surface it is working on.

13

PRICE LIST.

	Weight.	Deposition of Silv'r per hour.	Electrotyping. A Good Shell Obtained in 3 h'rs	Power consumed.	Price.
No. 1.	200 lbs.	25 ounces.	10 square feet.	1-3 horse power.	$200
" 2.	500 "	75 "	30 " "	1 " "	400
" 3.	1,300 "	225 "	100 " "	3 " "	750

Following are the addresses of some of the firms using these machines :

Messrs. Harper & Brothers, Franklin Square, N. Y., two No. 3.
   "   Smith & McDougal, 82 Beekman St., N. Y., No. 3.
   "   D. Appleton & Co., Works, Kent Avenue and Hewes Street, Brooklyn, E. D., No. 2.
Trow's Printing and Publishing Co., 205 to 213 Twelfth Street, New York, No. 2.
The Photo Engraving Co., 67 Park Place, No. 2.
Webster Manufacturing Company, Front Street, Brooklyn, Silver and Gold, No. 2.
American Nickel Plating Works, 118½ Milk Street, Boston Mass., Nickel, No. 2.
Mr. Herman Eckard, 14 and 16 Lorimer Street, Brooklyn, E. D., Nickel and Copper, No. 1.
Manhattan Silver Plate Co., corner Second Ave. and Twenty-second Street, New York, Silver, No. 1.
Keystone Silver Plate Co., 521 Cherry Street, Philadelphia, Silver, No. 1.
Branford Lock Works, Branford, Conn., Nickel and Brass, No. 1.
Messrs Nicholas Mueller's Sons, Courtlandt St., N. Y., Brass and Copper, No. 1.
New York Button Co., 73 Franklin St., N. Y., Nickel, No. 1.
Meriden Silver Plate Co., West Meriden, Conn., Silver, No. 1.

Acid.   **CHEMICALS.**   Per pound.
   Sulphuric..
   Nitric (chemically pure)..........................
   Nitric..
   Hydrochlaric......................................
   Acetic..
   Fuming Nitric.....................................
   Oxalic..
Ammonia..
Alcohol (per pint).................................
Sulphate of copper.................................
Sal ammoniac.......................................
14

Cyanide of potash.......................................
Bichromate of potash....................................
Nitrate of Potash.......................................
Sal soda..
Bicarbonate of soda.....................................
Cream tartar..
Bicarbonate potash......................................
Bisulphuret of carbon (per ounce).......................
Soldering acid, of our own manufacture (per bottle)...

ELECTRO-METALLURGY

PRACTICALLY TREATED.

152 Pages...............Price $1.25.

CONTENTS.

Discovery of Electrotyping.
Quantity and Intensity Electricity
Faraday's Nomenclature.
Constant Battery.
Various Forms of Battery.
Conducting Power of Solutions
Effects of Motion during Electro Deposition.
Electro Deposition of Copper.
Electrotyping Processes.
Preparation of Moulds.
Formulæ for Moulding Materials.
Bronzing Electrotypes.
Coating Iron with Copper.
Electro-Deposition of Silver.
Silver Solution.
"Bright" Plating.
Arrangement of Battery.
The Strength of Current Required for Different Metals.
Preparation of Work to be Plated.
Coating Lead or Pewter Surfaces.

Stripping Silver from Old Work, etc.
Recovering Silver from old Stripping Solutions, etc.
Deposition of Silver on non-Metallic Surfaces.
Electro Deposition of Gold.
Gold Solutions.
Preparation of Work to be Gilt.
Gilding Cheap Jewelry, etc.
Gilding Filigree Work, etc.
Electro Deposition of Brass and Bronze.
Brassing Solution.
Bronzing Solutions.
Electro - Brassing Cast - Iron Work.
Electro-Brassing Wrought-Iron Work.
Electro Deposition of Platinum and other Metals.
Electro Deposition of Zinc.
Preparation of Articles to be Coated.
Deposition of Alloys of Metals.

NAPIER'S ELECTRO METALLURGY.

PRICE $2.00.

Any Scientific Work published will be furnished at publisher's price.

THE HOCHHAUSEN
Dynamo Electric Machine
Nos. 1 and 2.

Below is a carefully prepared Price List of what a
Jeweller or Silver Plater ought to charge for

SILVER PLATING GOODS.

Single Articles.	Single.	D'ble.	Triple.
Soup Ladles.............................	$1 50	$2 25	$3 00
Tea Sets.................................	11 00	15 00	18 00
Coffee Pots.............................	2 50	3 50	4 50
Tea Pots.................................	2 00	3 00	4 00
Sugar Bowls.............................	1 75	2 00	2 50
Cream Cups.............................	1 00	1 50	2 00
Tea and Coffee Urns, small.............	4 50	6 50	9 00
Communion Sets........................	11 00	15 00	18 00
Ice Pitchers.............................	4 00	5 00	6 00
Wine and Milk Pitchers.................	3 00	3 50	4 00
Soup Tureens, small....................	5 00	6 50	9 00
Cake Baskets...........................	3 00	4 00	5 00
Card Baskets...........................	1 50	2 50	3 50
Fruit Stands............................	2 00	3 50	5 00
Celery Stands...........................	1 50	2 50	3 50
Wine Stands............................	3 00	4 50	5 50
Butter dishes...........................	2 50	3 00	3 75
Syrup Cups, with Waiters...............	1 75	2 00	3 00
Dining Castors.........................	2 50	3 50	5 00
Breakfast Castors.......................	1 50	2 00	3 00
Cups....................................	1 00	1 25	1 50
Soda Water Cups.......................	1 25	1 50	1 75
Call Bell...............................	75	1 25	1 50
Napkin Rings, per doz..................	3 00	4 50	6 50
Hunting Watch Cases...................	1 50	2 00	9 50
Open Face Watch Cases.................	1 25	1 75	2 25

KNIVES, FORKS, SPOONS, ETC.

Plain and Tipped, per doz.	Single.	D'ble.	Triple.
Tea, Egg, Mustard and Salt Spoons...	$1 75	$2 75	$3 75
Dessert Spoons and Forks	2 62	3 75	4 87
Table Spoons, Forks and Butter Knives	3 50	5 00	6 50
Oval Threaded and Beaded, additional	13	25	50
Figured Patterns, additional...........	25	50	75
Nut Picks	1 75	2 00	2 50
Table Knives, new	2 75	5 00	6 00
Dessert " "	3 00	4 00	5 00
Tea " "	2 50	3 50	4 50

The above warranted full plate as represented by weight.

Knives, forks and spoons, if badly scratched, are improved by
refinishing, before they are replated.   For this an extra charge
of $1.00 per dozen will be made.

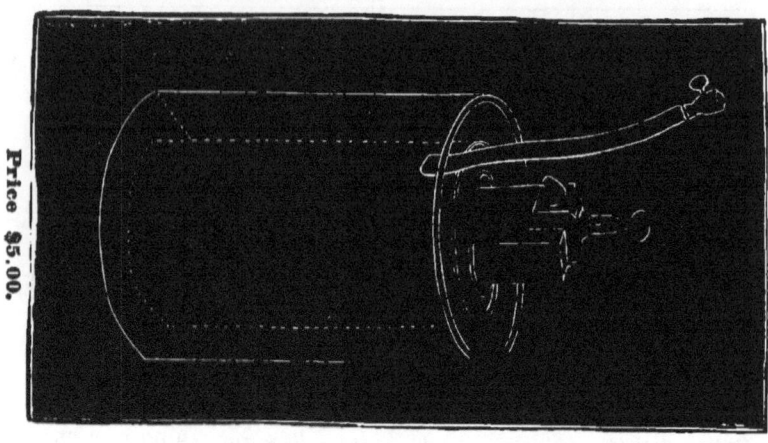
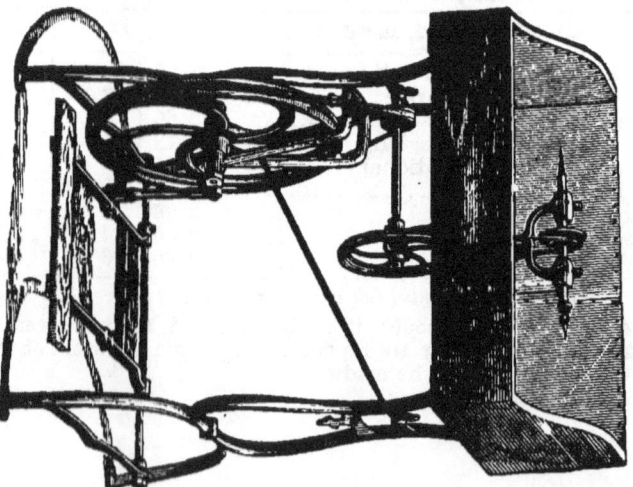